JUST ONE SEED

Original story by
Alma Flor Ada

English version by
Shirleyann Costigan

illustrated by
Frank Remkiewicz

 HAMPTON-BROWN BOOKS
Creative Materials for Active Learning™

Hampton-Brown Books
P. O. Box 223220
Carmel, California 93922

Printed in the United States of America

ISBN 1-56334-183-2

92 93 94 95 96 97 98 99 00 10 9 8 7 6 5 4 3 2 1

A seed is a gift
wrapped in a shell.
Plant it. Water it.
Care for it well.

"I will," said Miguel.

3

"That little seed
might grow a weed,"
said Dad.

"Wait and see,"
said Miguel.
And he planted
the seed.

4

"I really doubt that your
one little sprout
will grow," said Mom.

"Wait and see,"
said Miguel.
And he watered
the sprout.

5

"Good grief!
What's so important
about one little leaf?"
asked his brother.

"Wait and see,"
said Miguel.
And he pulled
up a weed.

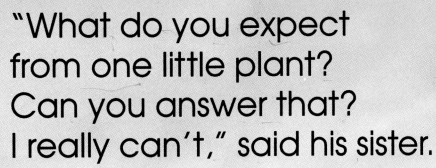

"What do you expect
from one little plant?
Can you answer that?
I really can't," said his sister.

"Wait and see,"
said Miguel.
And he
raked the soil.

7

Every day Miguel raked, watered, and waited.

8

Every day he weeded,
watered, and waited.

Until one day, he said,
"My plant has no flowers, and I've
waited so long. Tell me, little bird,
have I done something wrong?"

"Wait and see,"
said the bird.

Then, with the bird's help, the plant grew taller . . .

11

and taller . . .

12

and taller than tall,
until, WOW!

13

Out popped

a sunflower!

15